Never Play Music Right Next to the Zoo

To Ava, Axel, Archie, Ada, Esme, and Genevieve
—J. L.

For Laurent Linn, who helped me hit all the high notes!
—L. H.

SIMON & SCHUSTER BOOKS FOR YOUNG READERS · An imprint of Simon & Schuster Children's Publishing Division · 1230 Avenue of the Americas, New York, New York 10020 · Text copyright © 2013 by John Lithgow · Illustrations copyright © 2013 by Leeza Hernandez · All rights reserved, including the right of reproduction in whole or in part in any form. · SIMON & SCHUSTER BOOKS FOR YOUNG READERS is a trademark of Simon & Schuster, Inc. · For information about special discounts for bulk purchases, please contact Simon & Schuster Special Sales at 1-866-506-1949 or business@simonandschuster.com. · The Simon & Schuster Speakers Bureau can bring authors to your live event. For more information or to book an event, contact the Simon & Schuster Speakers Bureau at 1-866-248-3049 or visit our website at www.simonspeakers.com. · Book design by Laurent Linn · The text for this book is set in Joppa. · The illustrations for this book are rendered digitally. · Manufactured in China · 0813 SCP · 10   9   8   7   6   5   4   3   2   1 · Library of Congress Cataloging-in-Publication Data · Lithgow, John, 1945– · Never play music right next to the zoo / John Lithgow ; illustrated by Leeza Hernandez.—1st ed. · p. cm. · Summary: A concert gets out of hand when the animals at the neighboring zoo storm the stage and play the instruments themselves. · ISBN 978-1-4424-6743-9 (hardcover) · ISBN 978-1-4424-6744-6 (eBook) · 1. Children's songs, English—United States—Texts. [1. Concerts—Songs and music. 2. Orchestra—Songs and music. 3. Music—Songs and music. 4. Zoo animals—Songs and music. 5. Songs.] I. Hernandez, Leeza, ill. II. Title. · PZ8.3.L6375Ne 2013 · 782.42—dc23 · [E] · 2012013516

first edition

JOHN LITHGOW

Never Play Music Right Next to the Zoo

Illustrated by LEEZA HERNANDEZ

SIMON & SCHUSTER BOOKS FOR YOUNG READERS

New York   London   Toronto   Sydney   New Delhi

I went to a concert when I was a lad
no older than many of you.
I sat with my sister, my mother, my dad
at a band shell right next to the zoo.

The soft summer air was so balmy and sweet,

and the program was running so long,

that I found myself falling asleep in my seat,

despite all the music and song.

All at once the conductor

erupted with **rage!**

A band of wild animals

Oh, children! Remember!

Whatever you may do,

never play music right next to the zoo.

They'll burst from their cages, each beast and each bird,

desperate to play all the music they've heard.

The lions and the elephants, the bears and the raccoons will steal away the trumpets, the flutes, and bassoons.

replace the musicians, and chase them away.

Then they'll sit in the band shell and play.

The monkeys played fiddle, the bison played bass, the percussions were manned by the camel.

The **yak** played the **sax**

until red in the face—

a surprisingly musical mammal.

The **bonobo** played **oboe**, the **ferret** the **flute**, the **jackal** attacked the **bassoon**.

The hippo had chosen the **tuba** to toot, by the light of the silvery moon.

Siberian tigers,

Mongolian goats,

a **superabundance** of bestial notes!

As the animal orchestra filled up the air

with chaos,

confusion,

and

clatter,

the audience calmly continued to stare

as if nothing at all was the matter.

I trembled with terror, suppressing a scream,
while my parents just sat there enraptured.

Oh, how I wished it was only a dream
and those creatures all safely recaptured.

But since, by the minute, I'd grown less afraid,

I decided to sit back and watch while they played.

They finished and each put his instrument down,
then bowed and descended the stage.
Each shed his tuxedo (or evening gown)

and hurried back home to his cage.

Then each reminisced, so grateful and glad,

so full of contentment and pride.

My mother, meanwhile, strolled away with my dad,

but my sister remained by my side.

She **tugged** on my sweater and **spoke** in my ear:

Oh, children! **Remember!** Whatever you may do,

never play music right next to the zoo.

They'll **burst** from their cages, each **beast** and each **bird**, **desperate** to play all the music they've heard.

No, never play music right next to the zoo.

And pay **strict attention**

to rule **number two.**

Bear it in mind for the rest of your days:

Don't fall asleep when an orchestra plays.